"I'm not going in that dark place!" exclaimed Jason. He stood with his hands on his hips and stared at the dusty lane in front of him. Hairy trees draped themselves over the lane and blocked out the sun. An even darker-looking house sat at the end of the lane, framed by overgrown bushes and tangles of vines.

"Aw, Jason," Rudy gave his best friend a scornful look. "Do you want us to think you're a chicken or something?" He turned to his sister, "Come on, Alex!"

"Wait a minute," Alex stopped her younger brother. "Let me look around first. How did you ever find this creepy place?"

The ALEX Series
by Nancy Simpson Levene
- Shoelaces and Brussels Sprouts
- French Fry Forgiveness
- Hot Chocolate Friendship
- Peanut Butter and Jelly Secrets
- Mint Chocolate Miracles
- Cherry Cola Champions
- The Salty Scarecrow Solution
- Peach Pit Popularity
- T-Bone Trouble
- Grapefruit Basket Upset
- Apple Turnover Treasure

Apple Turnover Treasure

Nancy Simpson Levene

Chariot Books™

Chariot Books™ is an imprint of
David C. Cook Publishing Co.
David C. Cook Publishing Co., Elgin, Illinois 60120
David C. Cook Publishing Co., Weston, Ontario
Nova Distribution Ltd., Newton Abbot, England

APPLE TURNOVER TREASURE

Cover design by Bill Paetzold
Cover illustration by Neal Hughes

First Printing, 1992
Printed in the United States of America
98 97 96 95 94 7 6 5 4

Library of Congress Cataloging-in-Publication Data
Levene, Nancy S., 1949-
Apple turnover treasure / Nancy S. Levene
p.   cm.
Summary: Eleven-year-old Alex learns about heavenly
treasure as she gets to know a classmate and her family and
helps catch a group of bicycle thieves.
ISBN 1-55513-894-2
[1. Christian life—Fiction. 2. Conduct of life—Fiction.] I.
Title.
PZ7.L5724Ap 1992
[Fic]—dc20   91—45922
                                                    CIP
                                                    AC

CONTENTS

To Jesus
who puts a longing in my heart
for the things of heaven,
and enables me to see
that my real treasure is He
and
To Bridget Bieth
a number one ALEX fan!

Do not lay up for yourselves treasures upon earth,
where moth and rust destroy, and where thieves break
in and steal.
*   But lay up for yourselves treasures in heaven,*
where neither moth nor rust destroys, and where
thieves do not break in or steal; for where your
treasure is, there will your heart be also.
*   Matthew 6:19-21*
*   New American Standard Bible*

ACKNOWLEDGMENTS

Thank you, Peg Fawcett, for your advice on police matters; thank you, Bridget, for being such a neat ALEX fan; thank you Patti and Lara for your continued interest; and thank you, Cara, for the love and support you show for every ALEX book.

CHAPTER 1

A Dark House

"I'm not going in that dark place!" exclaimed Jason. He stood with his hands on his hips and stared at the dusty lane in front of him. Hairy trees draped themselves over the lane and blocked out the sun. An even darker-looking house sat at the end of the lane, framed by overgrown bushes and tangles of vines.

"Aw, Jason," Rudy gave his best friend a scornful look. "Do you want us to think you're a chicken or something?" He turned to his sister, "Come on, Alex!"

"Wait a minute," Alex stopped her younger brother. "Let me look around first. How did you ever find this creepy place?"

"I told you before," Rudy answered impatiently. "I passed by it on the way to soccer practice. Wait until you see the old house. It's awesome."

Alex ignored her brother and stared at the old stone wall lining either side of the lane. A rusty gate leaned against the wall, leaving the entrance to the lane open.

"It looks just like a place in a spooky movie," said Jason in a low voice.

Alex had to agree. She felt uneasy about walking down the dark lane to the house. Only its black outlines were visible against the pale October sky.

"Let's pull our bikes inside the gate," Alex suggested, stalling for time. Her nine-year-old brother, Rudy, had rushed home from soccer practice that afternoon all excited about some old house he had seen. Having nothing better to do, Alex had grabbed her bicycle and followed Rudy back to the old house. Rudy's best friend, Jason, had come along too.

They had ridden up and down several

neighborhood streets until they found the entrance to the old lane. It was well hidden behind two scraggly evergreen trees.

"I don't think we ought to go any further," Jason warned. "You never know who might be living in a house like that."

"Aw, come on, Jason," Rudy whined. "We'll just go a little ways down the lane."

"Well . . ." Jason shifted from one foot to the other.

"What do you say, Alex?" Rudy asked.

Alex took a deep breath and plunged forward down the lane. "Come on," she called back to Jason. "Rudy will never give up until we go see that house. It won't hurt just to look at it, I guess."

"All right!" Rudy grinned and went ahead with Alex. Jason hung back for just a moment but then hurried to join his friends. He did not want to stay behind by himself.

The children crept cautiously down the narrow lane. Even the leaves under their feet were silent—not crisp and crackling like fall leaves should be. They were limp and still. The air was heavy. Alex began to experience a closed-in feeling, as if she had somehow entered a different world.

"Don't be ridiculous!" she told herself. She tried to shrug off her uneasiness.

They moved on up the lane. Suddenly a loud crackling sounded from the bushes to the right of the path. Someone or something was coming their way!

For one scary moment, Alex couldn't speak. Then she found her voice.

"Quick!" she shouted to the boys. "Climb up a tree!"

Alex leapt into the nearest tree. She did not even notice its scratchy bark and sticky leaves. She noted with relief that Rudy had climbed into a tree across the lane, but she couldn't see Jason anywhere. Where was he?

For what seemed like ages, Alex clung silently to the tree. Just when she thought she could stand it no longer,

shrill voices broke the silence.

"I know I saw somebody down here," insisted a small child's voice.

"I thought I did too," another voice answered. It sounded a bit older and was definitely a girl's voice.

Inching around the trunk, Alex peeked out through the limbs of the tree. There, standing directly below her, was a small boy and a girl about her own age. Alex took a closer look at the girl. Why, it was Bridget Lyons, a new girl in her class at school!

Alex hesitated for a moment before calling down to Bridget. She didn't know Bridget very well, and she was sure Bridget would think she was an absolute goon perched up in a tree in the middle of this horrid place.

Finally, after clearing her throat, Alex called out as politely as she could, "Excuse me, uh, hi, Bridget!"

"Oh!" Bridget cried out in alarm. She and her young companion wheeled around to face Alex's tree.

"Uh, it's me. You know, Alex, from your class at school," Alex called again, trying to sound perfectly normal as she addressed Bridget from the top of a tree.

"Alex!" Bridget responded. "What are you doing up in that tree?"

"Well," Alex tried to explain, "When I heard you coming, I guess I got a little scared and climed up in this tree to hide"

Bridget laughed. "Well, come on down out of the tree now. It's just me and my brother, Peter."

Swinging herself out of the tree, Alex dropped to the ground beside Bridget and the little boy. Things seemed much different in the lane now. Although it was still shady, the lane did not seem frightening anymore. It was just old and rather shabby.

"Uh, I guess you live close by here," said Alex to Bridget, not knowing what else to say.

"Oh, yes," replied Bridget. "This is our

property. We live in the house at the end of the lane. This is my brother, Peter."

"Hi," Alex said to the little boy. That reminded her that she, too, had a brother and that he was hiding somewhere close by. She stared up into the trees on the other side of the lane. She could just barely see Rudy peeking out from behind one of the thick tree trunks.

"Come on, Rudy. You can come down now!" she hollered.

Bridget and Peter gasped in surprise as Rudy slid down out of the tree.

"This is my brother, Rudy," Alex introduced him to Bridget and Peter. "And somewhere around here is his best friend."

Alex scanned all the trees in the area. There was still no sign of Jason.

"JASON!" Alex called. "JASON! WHERE ARE YOU?"

A loud, rustling sound behind Alex startled her. She turned to see Jason crawl out of a tangle of bushes on his hands and knees. He was a mess! His hair and shoulders were covered with moss, dried leaves, and twigs, and his shirt was torn in several places.

"What happened to you?" Alex cried.

"I think I got into a patch of thorns," Jason replied, rubbing his arms and trying to brush off the leaves with his hands.

"Brussels sprouts!" Alex laughed at Jason. She and the others helped him brush off the leaves and twigs. Soon the once dark lane was full of laughing, chattering voices.

"Would you like to come up to the house?" Bridget invited Alex and the boys.

"Oh, yeah," Alex answered right away. Now they could see the old house up close. She hoped Rudy and Jason would not say how creepy they had thought the house looked.

When they reached the house, Alex bit her lip to keep from saying what she really thought of it. It looked absolutely dreadful. It was dark and monstrous. Some of the windows were covered with black sheets of plastic. The big front porch looked worn and was missing several steps. The whole house seemed to stare down at Alex with a tired frown.

"Come on in," Bridget beckoned them.

Alex, Rudy, and Jason followed Bridget and Peter over a rough gravel path to the front porch. They had to jump over gaping holes left by missing front steps.

Alex's uneasy feelings returned. Should they go into the house? Her parents had always told her never to go into strange places, and this was certainly a strange-looking house. What would she find inside?

Hanging back a little and moving close to Rudy and Jason, Alex whispered, "Be ready to run if I say so." The boys nodded and followed her across the creaky porch.

Bridget held a door open for them. "Go on in," she urged.

Alex took a deep breath and stepped through the door.

CHAPTER 2

Shattered Glass

To her surprise, Alex stepped inside a large, cheery kitchen that smelled distinctly of cinnamon. There were clean, white walls and a shiny floor. A red and white tablecloth brightened a large table set in front of a double set of windows. The appearance of the room was such a contrast to the gloomy outside of the house that Alex's fears left, and she began to relax.

At the kitchen table sat two young girls. They looked exactly alike. They both had long, double sets of gleaming brown pigtails streaming down their backs. And they both munched on the most gooey and delicious-looking apple turnovers Alex had ever seen.

"These are my twin sisters, Sarah and Sandra," said Bridget, pointing to the girls.

"Brussels sprouts!" Alex exclaimed. "I thought we had a big family with three children at our house, but you beat us with four."

"Five," Bridget corrected Alex with a smile. "My baby brother, Michael, is at the sitter's. Mom will pick him up on her way home from work."

"You mean your mom is at work?" Alex asked. It seemed strange to be in a house full of children with no grown-up around. "Who takes care of all of you?" Alex wanted to know.

"I do," Bridget replied simply. She waved Alex and the boys to chairs around the table. "Would you like an apple turnover?" she asked them. "I just made a fresh batch before I went outside."

"You mean you can make apple turnovers?" Alex asked in surprise. "I'm impressed!" she added.

"Oh, it's nothing," Bridget shrugged. "Just a little flour, sugar, and apple pie filling. Of course, I sprinkle cinnamon sugar on the outside. Here, let me warm some up for you."

Amazed, Alex watched as Bridget quickly popped a pan full of turnovers into the oven. After a minute or two, she served them warm and gooey to Alex and the boys.

"Yummy!" the children cried after one bite.

"Do you cook a lot?" Alex asked Bridget.

"Oh, yeah," Bridget answered. "I always make dinner because Mom does not have time with working and trying to take care of five children."

Just then a clear bell rang from somewhere outside the kitchen. Alex, Rudy, and Jason jumped at the noise.

"What was that?" all three asked.

"Oh, it's just Grandpa," Bridget laughed at the worried look on their faces.

"Come on, you can meet my grandpa." She put an extra turnover on a plate and led the children out of the kitchen.

They followed Bridget past a dimly lit dining room and into a darkened living room. Alex stared at the enormous rooms and high ceilings. The rooms did not contain much furniture, and the emptiness made them look even bigger. On the other side of the living room, a hallway led them to a bedroom at the back of the house.

Peeking inside the bedroom, Alex saw a big brass bed covered with several layers of faded quilts. A little, old, white-haired man poked his head out from underneath the covers. He grinned at Alex from across the room.

"Look, Grandpa," Bridget said as she entered the room, "I've brought you an apple turnover."

"Oh, my very favorite!" exclaimed the old man. He smiled at Bridget as she set the plate down on a table beside the bed.

"These are my friends from school, Grandpa," said Bridget, pointing to Alex, Rudy, and Jason.

"Come closer, children, and let me get a better look at you," the old man asked in a high-pitched, quavering voice. Alex, Rudy, and Jason moved closer to the bed.

"Now, tell me your names and where you're from," said the old man.

As Alex introduced herself and the two boys, she decided that she liked this old man very much. His smile was bright, and his eyes twinkled as he looked at each one of them.

"Rudy!" the old man exclaimed when Alex introduced her brother. "Now that's a name I haven't heard in years!"

"It's not his real name," Alex quickly added.

"It is, too!" Rudy protested.

"It's just his nickname," explained Alex.

"Well, it's a real nickname!" insisted Rudy.

The old man laughed. "It's a very good nickname," he told Rudy. "When I was a boy, I had a best friend named Rudy."

"Really?" Rudy was delighted. He moved closer to the bed.

"Yes, I had a friend named Rudy," the old man repeated with a faraway look in his eyes. Then he said, "But my friend Rudy looked more like your friend Jason. He had red hair and freckles." Jason smiled shyly at the old man.

"Why did you ring your bell, Grandpa?" Bridget asked.

"Oh, yes," Grandpa smiled. "All this wonderful company almost made me forget." He winked at Alex. "Would you mind bringing me a small glass of water?" he asked Bridget.

"Of course, Grandpa," Bridget replied. She hurried off to get the water. When she returned, Bridget placed a glass of water on a small table beside the bed.

"Good-bye," the children called as they followed Bridget out of the room.

"Good-bye," Grandpa replied. "Please come again."

Back in the kitchen, Alex asked Bridget, "Is your grandpa sick? Why is he in bed?"

"Oh, he's not really sick," Bridget answered. "He just can't get out of bed. You see, he had a bad fall a few weeks ago and broke his hip. Ever since then, he hasn't been able to walk."

"How come?" Rudy asked. He liked the kindly old man.

"It just happens with old people," Bridget tried to explain. "Their bones don't heal very fast and once they get down in bed, it's hard for them to get up. He may never walk again."

"Oh, how awful!" the others were concerned. They liked Grandpa very much.

"Yeah, it is sad," Bridget agreed. "In the last few years, Grandpa hasn't been in very good health. As you can see, he hasn't been able to keep up this house very well. Then after he broke his hip, he couldn't do anything. So our family decided to move in with him and take care of him. We've only lived here a few weeks."

Alex was about to reply when suddenly a sound like shattering glass came from a nearby room.

"What was that?" Alex asked in alarm.

"Oh, no, not again!" Bridget wailed. She ran into the next room. The other children followed her. They all stopped to stare at a broken dining room window.

"How did that happen?" Alex exclaimed, coming to stand beside Bridget.

"This is how it happened," Bridget said angrily. She bent down and picked up a rock. She placed the rock in Alex's hands.

"Brussels sprouts, you mean somebody threw a rock in the window?" Alex asked, wide-eyed with surprise.

"Yes," Bridget nodded. "A couple of older boys have been coming around here and throwing rocks at our windows. They have broken two other windows."

"But why would they do such a thing?" Alex wanted to know.

Bridget shrugged. "Grandpa says they do it because boys like to throw rocks at old, abandoned houses."

"But this house is not abandoned," said Alex.

"Yeah, but it kind of looks like it from the outside," Bridget pointed out.

Alex thought about how dark and spooky looking the old house had seemed when she and the boys had first seen it.

"Well, why don't we go outside and tell them that people live here?" Rudy suggested.

"No, we can't do that," Bridget answered quickly. "My mom doesn't want any of us to go outside when those boys are around."

"Yeah," Alex agreed, "they might start throwing rocks at us. Have you seen what the boys look like?" she asked Bridget.

"Yes, I've seen them from a distance," Bridget replied. "I never got a real good look at their faces though."

"Let's take a look now," Alex suggested. She crawled over to the broken window, carefully avoiding any broken glass on the floor, and ducked under the windowsill. Bridget and the boys joined her. Slowly, they raised their heads to peek out of the bottom half of the broken window. A long-haired boy stood several feet away. He was partially hidden by the trees. His companion was nowhere in sight. As they watched, the boy bent over and picked up something from the ground.

"Let's get away from these windows in case he throws another rock," Bridget suggested. "I'm going to call my mom at work."

The children moved back into the kitchen. They kept well away from the windows. It was scary to think that at

any moment a rock might come sailing
through the glass.

Bridget picked up the telephone and
dialed her mother's number. Alex
listened as Bridget told her mother what
had happened.

"What did your mom say?" Alex asked
Bridget when she hung up the phone.

"Oh, she's calling the police," Bridget
answered.

"The police!" the children exclaimed.

Before anyone could say another word,

a second rock exploded through one of the kitchen windows. The children dove under the big kitchen table and huddled close together. Sarah and Sandra began to cry.

"I can't believe they did it again!" Alex exclaimed.

"They've never broken two windows at once," exclaimed Bridget.

"Why don't we pray that they don't throw any more rocks?" suggested Alex.

"Good idea," Bridget agreed.

The children bowed their heads.

"Dear Lord Jesus," Alex prayed, "please don't let those boys throw any more rocks through the windows today. We pray in Your name. Amen."

"Amen," the others echoed.

"I feel better," Alex declared after the prayer.

"Me, too," agreed the others.

They waited quietly under the kitchen table for the police to arrive.

CHAPTER 3

Stolen Bicycles

The loud crunch of gravel outside announced the arrival of a car. Heavy footsteps sounded on the front porch. A loud knocking pounded on the kitchen door.

"POLICE!" someone shouted.

Bridget ran to open the door. Two police officers stood outside. Their faces softened as soon as they saw the frightened group of children inside.

"Please come in," Bridget held the door open. The two officers, a man and a woman, stepped inside. Sarah and Sandra ran to hide behind Bridget's back.

"Is your mother at home?" one of the police officers asked in a kindly voice. She was a young-looking officer with blonde, curly hair. Alex liked her right away.

"No, my mother called you from work," Bridget answered, "but she's on her way home right now."

"Please tell us what happened," the young officer asked.

The children showed the officers the rocks and the damaged windows in the kitchen and in the dining room. They told them about the two boys who had thrown the rocks. By that time, Bridget's mother arrived home with her youngest child, one-year-old Michael.

From the moment she saw her, Alex liked Mrs. Lyons. Like Bridget, she was small and pretty, if just a bit tired looking. She had lots of dark, bouncy curls. As she talked to the police officers, Alex decided that Bridget and her mother looked quite a bit alike.

"Hey, Alex, look what time it is!" Rudy suddenly pointed at the kitchen clock. "Mom's gonna wonder where we are."

"Brussels sprouts!" Alex exclaimed. "I had no idea it was almost six o'clock. We better get home fast!"

Alex, Rudy, and Jason said good-bye to Bridget and the others.

"Say good-bye to Grandpa for us," Rudy called to Bridget as he ran down the gravel drive after Alex and Jason.

"Please come back again," Bridget shouted after them. "Maybe we can do more than hide under the table!"

The children ran all the way down the lane. As she ran, Alex thought, *We better pedal fast. With my new ten-speed, I could probably make it home before six, but I don't think the boys could keep up.* Rudy and Jason each had short dirt bikes, and no matter how fast they pedaled, they could not match the speed of Alex's racing bike. Alex was very proud of her bicycle. She had saved her money and paid for half of it herself. Her parents had matched the other half.

Looking forward to jumping on her

bicycle and racing home, Alex rushed back to the old stone fence and the rusty gate. When she got there, she discovered that something terrible had happened. The boys knew it too. They stopped still and stared at one another.

"OUR BIKES ARE GONE!" they all cried at once.

Running in all directions, the children searched for the missing bikes. They checked a huge clump of weeds to the left of the lane. They looked in the tangled growth of bushes on either side of the gate. They even checked the sidewalk in front of the entrance to the lane. The bicycles were nowhere to be seen.

"Oh, no," Alex moaned and sank to the ground, her head in her hands. "What am I going to do? My beautiful racing bike is gone!"

"Alex," Rudy tapped her on the shoulder. "Shouldn't we call Mom or something?"

"Call Mom?" Alex looked at her broth-

er in a daze. She shook her head to clear her thoughts. "Yeah, we'd better call her," Alex agreed. "We better go back to Bridget's house." She turned to go and then stopped. "Hey! Wait a minute!" she exclaimed. "Let's go tell the police officers that our bikes were stolen. Come on!"

The three children ran as fast as they could back up the lane. They reached the house just as the two police officers were getting into the patrol car.

"Wait! Please wait!" Alex cried. She ran

to the car. "Our bikes have been stolen!"

"What bikes?" one of the officers asked. "We saw no bicycles when we drove up to the house."

"But we rode them here," Alex insisted, "and now they're gone! And mine was a brand-new ten-speed that I bought with my own money!"

With that, the police officers climbed back out of the car and began to question the children about their bicycles. Rudy and Jason helped Alex give a full description of each bike.

"We will report the theft and look for your bikes," the officers said, "but don't get your hopes up. We usually do not find stolen bicycles."

After the police officers had gone, Alex telephoned her mother and explained everything that had happened.

Her father rushed over to Bridget's house. He shook his head when he saw the damage that the rocks had done to the windows. He helped Bridget's mother secure pieces of boards and plastic over the broken windows. It was quite dark before they got in the car to drive home.

"I'm sorry about your new bicycle, Firecracker," Father called Alex by her nickname.

"Yeah," said Alex sadly. "If only I hadn't left it at the gate. If only I had brought it up to the house."

Father nodded. "Sometimes we learn the hard way."

"But what kind of person would steal somebody's bike?" Alex cried out in anger.

"I bet it was those boys who threw the rocks," Rudy decided.

"Yeah, if I ever see them again, they'll be sorry!" Alex exploded.

"If those boys are not afraid to throw rocks at windows and steal bicycles, it would not be a wise idea to mess around with them," warned Father.

"You mean you want to just let them get away with stealing our bikes?" Alex asked in surprise.

"No, but I'd rather let the police handle it," answered Father.

"But the police said that they hardly ever recover stolen bicycles," Alex protested.

"I know," Father thought for a moment. "I wish we knew the names of the boys. Did you recognize them from school?"

"No," Alex said glumly. "I think they're a lot older than me. Say, I wonder if Barbara might know them." Barbara was Alex's older sister. She was almost sixteen years old and in high school.

"That's an idea," Father agreed. "Why don't you tell Barbara about the boys and see if she might know who they are?"

As soon as they reached home, Alex ran up to her sister's bedroom. As usual, Barbara was talking on the telephone. She hung up rather quickly, however, when she saw the anxious look on Alex's face.

"What's the matter with you?" Barbara asked Alex.

Alex told her what had happened that afternoon. She asked Barbara if she might know who the boys were.

"No," Barbara replied. "None of my friends would do that!" She thought for a moment. "Of course, there are some boys in our school who might do something like that. Every school seems to have a few bad ones."

"Who are the bad ones at your school?" Alex asked eagerly. She was ready to confront the boys that very night.

"Well, let's see," Barbara frowned, "There's Jake Thomas and Randy Zoeller and Bobby Kellogg and . . ."

"Wait a minute!" Alex interrupted. "Can we look them up in your last year's yearbook? Maybe I would recognize one of them."

"Oh, sure," Barbara pulled a thick book off her shelf and handed it to Alex.

Alex traced the gold lettering on the cover with her finger. It read, "Kingswood High School." Even though this was

Barbara's sophomore year, Alex still had trouble believing that her sister was really in high school.

Barbara and Alex poured through page after page of pictures in the yearbook. Barbara pointed out the boys most likely to have stolen the bicycles.

Alex stared at the pictures but finally had to admit that she could not positively identify the boys.

"I only got to see one of them for a second through the window," Alex told her sister, "but maybe Bridget might recognize them. She's seen them a few times. Could I take your yearbook to her house tomorrow?"

"Why not invite Bridget over here tomorrow?" Barbara suggested. "I'd rather you did not take my yearbook out of the house."

"But Bridget can't come over here. Her mother works and she has to take care of her little brother and sisters and her grandpa," Alex explained.

"Really?" Barbara was amazed. "That's a lot of responsibility for an eleven year old to handle."

"Yeah," Alex agreed, "and that's not all. Bridget has to cook dinner, too!"

"Wow," Barbara shook her head. "I guess we've got it easy compared to Bridget."

"I don't think she really minds," Alex said thoughtfully. "She seems to like doing things for her family." Alex stood up to leave the room. "Can I take your yearbook over to Bridget's house tomorrow?" she asked her sister again. "I'll be real careful with it."

"Okay," Barbara agreed, "but don't let it get messed up."

The next day after school, Alex walked to Bridget's house. She carried Barbara's yearbook under her arm.

"Brussels sprouts, this thing gets heavy," Alex told Bridget as she dropped the book onto Bridget's kitchen table.

"It is pretty big," Bridget agreed, picking up the yearbook. She and Alex opened the book and began to look at pictures of high school boys.

"Hey, there's my sister's picture," Alex cried. She pointed out Barbara's picture to Bridget.

"Oh, she's really pretty!" Bridget exclaimed.

"Yeah," Alex agreed. "She gets her blonde hair from Mom. I guess I look more like Dad." Alex twisted a few strands of her brown hair through her fingers and sighed.

The girls continued their search through Barbara's yearbook. They looked at the pictures in every class. Finally, Bridget sighed, "I'm just not sure I can identify them. There are several boys that kind of look like them, but I've never seen them up close."

Alex was disappointed. She desperately wanted to recover her bicycle. She had hoped that Bridget could identify the thieves.

"I guess we'll just have to wait until they come back and then try to get a better look at them," Alex finally decided.

Almost every day after school, Alex walked home with Bridget and her small brother and sisters. Sometimes Rudy and Jason would join them.

Alex got to know Bridget and her family very well. She especially liked to hear Grandpa tell stories about the days when he was a young boy. The world seemed more simple back then. All Grandpa had cared about was what kind of bait to use with his fishing pole.

Alex also liked to watch Bridget take care of her younger brother and sisters. She marveled at Bridget's ability to cook, and she agreed with Grandpa that Bridget's apple turnovers were the best she had ever eaten.

Bridget would laugh and look pleased. One day she told Alex, "I have always helped Mom take care of the twins, ever since they were born. Then when Daddy died and Michael was only a few weeks old, I had to really take charge because Mom had to go to work."

"But isn't it hard on you sometimes?" Alex asked, concerned for the friend she had come to love.

"Naw, it's okay," Bridget smiled at Alex. "Mom says that even though we don't possess many worldly things, we're storing up great heavenly treasure instead."

"Heavenly treasure?" Alex repeated. "What do you mean?"

"Well, it says in the Bible that you should store up treasure in heaven rather than treasure on earth," Bridget explained. "Mom says that we all have our own treasure chests in heaven, and every time you do something good for someone else, God puts more treasure in your treasure chest. Then when you get to heaven, you have a whole pile of heavenly treasure just waiting for you."

"Brussels sprouts, that's neat!" exclaimed Alex.

"Yeah, and no one can ever take it away from you because God is the one who's saving it for you," added Bridget.

"Not like a bicycle," Alex frowned at the memory of her recently stolen bike.

"No, not at all like a bicycle," Bridget agreed and gave Alex a sad pat on the shoulder.

CHAPTER 4

Buried Treasure

That evening at the dinner table, Alex surprised her family by saying to Barbara, "Don't bother clearing the table. I'll be glad to do it tonight." Before Barbara could reply, Alex had whisked all the plates, bowls, and glasses to the kitchen.

Then when Rudy was getting ready to rinse the dishes to put them in the dishwasher, Alex offered, "I'll take your turn tonight and rinse the dishes."

"Does that mean I have to take your turn tomorrow night?" Rudy asked suspiciously.

"No, I'll do it for free," Alex smiled and took the plate from his hand.

When Father bundled the trash together, Alex grabbed the sack from his hand and started to carry it out.

"Wait a minute," Father stopped her, a puzzled look on his face. "Why are you so eager to do other people's chores tonight, Firecracker?" he asked.

"Oh, I'm just trying to fill up my treasure chest in heaven," Alex replied.

"You're trying to do what?" Father looked even more surprised.

"Well, Bridget's mom said that whenever you do something good for someone else, God puts treasure into your treasure chest in heaven. Then when you get to heaven, you have a chest full of heavenly treasure waiting for you."

Father smiled and put his arm around Alex. "You know, I think Bridget's mother is right about that. I like that idea so much I think I'll use it for my next Treasure Hunt lesson."

Sure enough, when the next Tuesday rolled around, Father put on his captain's sea hat with the red plume and cried, "Look alive, buccaneers! We're going on a real treasure hunt tonight! There's buried treasure to find!"

"Brussels sprouts, that's neat!" exclaimed Alex. Of course she always loved Treasure Hunt nights. Every Tuesday the family would get together to learn a story from the Bible. As they discussed the story, they would discover messages from God. Those messages would be the treasure they hunted. But tonight promised to be extra exciting. Tonight they were going to have a real treasure hunt!

"Before we begin our search for treasure," Father held up his hands for quiet, "I want to read you something that Jesus said about treasure in heaven. It is found in the book of Matthew, chapter 6, verses 19 to 21. Here is what Jesus said:

"Do not lay up for yourselves treasures upon earth, where moth and rust destroy, and where thieves break in and steal. But lay up for yourselves treasures in heaven, where neither moth nor rust destroys, and where thieves do not break in or steal; for where your treasure is, there will your heart be also."

When Father finished reading, he asked, "What do you think Jesus meant when He talked about treasures in heaven?"

"He was talking about treasure that God saves up for you so that when you get to heaven, you'll have it," answered Alex.

"Is this treasure in heaven like treasure on earth?" Father asked. "Is it money and jewels, or gold and silver?"

"No," Alex replied. "It's much better than that."

"How do you know?" questioned Father.

"It has to be," Alex told him. "If it's God's treasure, it has to be better."

"You're right, Firecracker," Father smiled. "Heavenly treasure is much more valuable than earthly treasure.

For one thing, it's eternal. It's not like earthly treasure that rusts or gets eaten up by moths or is stolen. Heavenly treasure lasts forever. Jesus said that we should store up heavenly treasure for ourselves. How do you think we can do that?" Father asked his children.

"By loving other people and doing good things for them," Alex answered again.

"That's right, Firecracker," said Father. "You get an A+ in this lesson. There are many ways to help people. In Matthew 25:35, 36, Jesus told us some specific ways that we can help people. He said we should feed and clothe the poor, be kind to strangers, visit the sick, and visit people in prison. Jesus said that whenever we do one of those things for a person on earth, God counts it as if we had done it for Jesus Himself."

"Really?" Rudy was surprised. "You mean that whenever I go in to visit Bridget's grandpa, it's like I'm going in to visit Jesus?"

"Yes," Father smiled. "You can imagine that it's Jesus lying in that bed because that's the way it is counted in heaven."

"Hey, that's like a double bonus," cried Alex. "When you do something good for someone, God counts it as if you did it for Jesus, and He also puts a piece of treasure in your treasure chest!"

"Very good, Firecracker," Father laughed. "I have another question for you. What did Jesus mean when He said, 'For where your treasure is, there will your heart be also?'"

"I think I can answer that," said Barbara. "If you store treasure in heaven, then you will think of heaven as your permanent home. Your heart will always look toward heaven. But if you only store up treasure on earth, you will want to stay on earth with your treasure and you might not make it to heaven at all."

"That's exactly right," Father smiled at his oldest daughter. "I couldn't have said it better." He stood up and fished a few folded-up pieces of paper from out of his pockets.

"Is everyone ready for the treasure hunt?" Father asked with a grin.

"YEAH!" hollered Alex and Rudy.

Father passed out a slip of paper to each child. "Here are your first clues. Follow them to the next clues. Each clue will lead you to another one and eventually to the buried treasure. Are you ready? On your mark, get set, GO!"

Alex hurriedly unfolded her slip of paper. It said, "Clue Number One." On it was written:

CLUE NO. 2 CAN BE FOUND IN SOMETHING YOU USE ON THE MOUND.

Alex thought for a moment. "On the mound" had to mean the pitcher's mound. Alex was the pitcher for her softball team. And what else would she use on the mound but her pitcher's glove?

"Come on, boy!" Alex called to T-Bone, the family labrador. The big, black dog had been sitting by Alex with his chin resting on her knees. He and Alex clattered up the stairs to her room. She grabbed her glove off a hook on the wall and stuck her hand inside. Her fingers immediately pulled out a piece of paper that read, "Clue Number Two." It pointed the way to clue number three and said:

IF YOU WANT TO FIND CLUE NO. 3 YOU HAVE TO CLIMB UP IN ME.

"What?" Alex exclaimed. "What does that mean?" She sat down on her bed to think. "Let's see, T-Bone," she said to the dog. What are things that I climb? I climb fences and trees. Hey! I bet it's up in the tree house!"

Alex and T-Bone raced back down the stairs and outside to the backyard. Alex quickly climbed the tree that she had climbed so many times before. Poor T-Bone had to stay at the bottom of the tree. He barked his disappointment as he watched Alex climb the tree without him.

Upon entering the tree house, Alex found clue number three taped to an inside wall. It read:

LOOK FOR CLUE NO. 4
AND DO NOT MOAN,
IT'S FOUND IN SOMETHING
WHERE CLOTHES ARE THROWN.

"It's gotta be the laundry hamper," Alex decided when she had read the clue. Climbing back down the tree, Alex called to the dog, "Come on, T-Bone, we gotta go back upstairs to the laundry hamper."

Alex and T-Bone ran upstairs to the bathroom. Throwing open the lid, Alex discovered clue number four on top of the clothes piled inside the laundry hamper. It read:

THIS IS YOUR LAST CLUE
NOW DON'T BE BLUE
DIG BY THE WOODPILE
THERE IS TREASURE FOR YOU.

"Come on, boy. We gotta go outside again," Alex told T-Bone who was happily sniffing the dirty clothes in the

laundry hamper. He tore himself away
to follow after Alex as she clumped back
down the stairs.

Alex and T-Bone ran for the woodpile.
They found Father and Mother waiting
for them. Father was holding a shovel.

"Congratulations, Firecracker,"
chuckled Father. "You were the first one
to finish. Here is a shovel. You can dig
for your treasure right over here."
Father pointed to a spot behind the
woodpile that had been covered over

with freshly turned dirt.

Alex took the shovel and began to dig. Rudy and Barbara soon joined her. Before long, Alex's shovel hit something besides dirt. She knelt down and scooped the dirt away. It was a shoe box.

"Hey!" she cried. "I think I've found my treasure!"

Rudy and Barbara crowded around Alex as she pulled the shoe box from the dirt. Opening the lid, Alex found a bundle of newspaper folded around something soft. What could it be? Alex tore off the newspaper and held up her treasure.

It was one of Mother's cleaning rags. It was full of holes. It looked like T-Bone had played a game of tug-of-war with the rag. Pinned to the rag was a note that read, "Sorry! The moths ate your treasure."

"Brussels sprouts!" Alex exclaimed. She frowned at Father. Rudy and Barbara laughed.

Next, it was Barbara's turn to dig for treasure. "I think I've found something," she soon announced. Alex and Rudy joined her as she pulled another shoe box from the dirt.

Opening the lid, she found an old, rusty tin can. A note taped to it read, "Sorry! Your treasure has rusted!"

"Oh, Dad!" Barbara laughed. She playfully tossed the tin can at her father.

"Well, we still have to dig for my treasure," Rudy reminded the others. They all gathered around Rudy as he dug with the shovel. He dug and dug. Finally the shovel hit a third shoe box. He quickly tore off the lid.

"Oh, no!" he hollered. His shoe box was empty except for a note. It read, "Sorry! Thieves have stolen your treasure!"

Alex and Barbara laughed at the surprised look on Rudy's face. He turned to Father and asked, "What kind of treasure is this?"

Father laughed and answered, "That's earthly treasure. Jesus said not to save up earthly treasure for ourselves because it could be eaten by moths, rust, or be stolen by thieves. Instead, we are to store up heavenly treasure." Father pulled out another box from behind one end of the woodpile. "Heavenly Treasure" was written on the lid.

Father opened the box and handed each of his children a small package. A message was taped to each package. The message on Alex's package said, "Well done, good and faithful servant. You have been kind to strangers."

Alex opened the package. Inside was a large chocolate candy bar. "Ummmmm, yummy!" Alex cried when she saw it.

Barbara and Rudy opened their packages. The note on Barbara's package said, "Well done, good and faithful servant. You have given to the poor." Rudy's note said, "Well done, good and faithful servant. You have visited the sick."

Rudy was delighted. "I'm glad I visited Grandpa so much," he exclaimed as he bit into his candy bar.

The others laughed.

"Just remember that this candy bar only represents your heavenly treasure," Father reminded Rudy. "God is saving your real heavenly treasure for you."

"Yeah, and whatever it is, you know it's gotta be better than anything we can get on earth," Alex added.

CHAPTER 5

Trailing the Thieves

The next day after school, Alex brought her friends Janie, Julie, and Lorraine to Bridget's house. The girls were eager to see the old house and meet Bridget's family.

Alex and Bridget had begun a new project and needed their friends to help. They had decided to clean and fix up an old porch on the back side of the house for Grandpa. The porch was entirely enclosed with glass. Alex and Bridget were sure that once the glass was cleaned, the room would sparkle with sunshine.

"Let's call it the sun room," Alex suggested that afternoon as the five girls munched on Bridget's apple turn-overs before settling down to work.

"Great idea," replied Bridget. "Grandpa will love to sit in here and look out at his yard and flowers. Of course, he will only be able to come to the sun room if we get him a wheelchair," Bridget added sadly. "None of us is strong enough to carry him this far."

"Are you going to get him a wheelchair?" Alex asked.

"We're trying to save up for one," Bridget replied, "but wheelchairs are really expensive. I don't know if we'll ever get the money."

"Well, how about praying about it?" suggested Alex. "Let's pray right now so God can be working on it while we work on the room." She knelt down and bowed her head. The other girls joined her on the floor of the sun room.

"Dear Lord Jesus," Alex prayed, "please help Grandpa to get a wheelchair. We pray in Your name. Amen."

The girls worked hard on the sun room. They knocked cobwebs out of the corners and swept up piles of dust from the floor. They had to cart a collection of old, collapsed furniture outside before they could even start to clean the windows. Scrubbing the windows was no easy chore. The girls had to go over and over them with soap and water to get them clean. Bridget's mother bought the girls a can of paint, and they carefully painted the woodwork and trim around the windows a dazzling white.

Finally, one day the job was done. Alex and Bridget gazed at the sun room with pride. It looked better than they had ever imagined possible. The windows shone and everything looked crisp and sparkling clean.

"Brussels sprouts!" Alex exclaimed. "This room looks fantastic!"

"I think it's the best room in the house," Bridget declared.

"Let's move in the furniture," Alex

suggested excitedly. They had found a sofa and chairs upstairs in an unused room. Bridget's mother had said they could use the furniture in the sun room.

"Do you think we can move the furniture all by ourselves?" Bridget asked Alex as she led the way upstairs.

"Oh, sure," Alex waved her hand. "All we have to do is let it kind of slide down the stairs one step at a time. It'll be easy."

Alex was right about the chairs. It was fairly easy for the two girls to haul them down the stairs. The sofa, however, was another matter. They managed to slide it down several steps but came to a halt as soon as they reached a sharp bend in the stairway. They pushed with all their might, but they could not get the sofa around the bend.

"Maybe if we turn it on its side, we can pull it through," Alex suggested. She was on the bottom end of the sofa, which was the heaviest end to carry.

"We can try," Bridget sounded doubtful.

The girls tipped the sofa as far on its side as they could manage and tried to drag it around the bend.

"Oh, come on!" Alex yanked and pulled with all her strength, but it was no use. They sofa would not budge. In fact, it was now so tightly wedged against the railing that it could not be moved forward or backward.

"Brussels sprouts," Alex sighed in frustration. She wearily sat down on a step.

"Now what do we do?" Bridget moaned. "I'm stuck up here! I can't get down past the sofa."

"Why not crawl over the sofa?" Alex suggested.

"Okay," replied Bridget. She put one foot up on the sofa and stopped. "What if it starts sliding down the stairs while I'm on top of it?" she worried.

"Are you kidding?" Alex exclaimed. "This thing isn't going anywhere!"

"My mother's going to love this,"
Bridget grumbled as she carefully
balanced on top of the sofa. "Now we
have to climb over the sofa just to get up
and down the stairs."

Alex started to laugh at Bridget's
comment, but at that moment a loud
shattering of glass sounded from down-
stairs.

"Those boys are throwing rocks
through the windows again!" Bridget
cried. With one big leap, she was over

the sofa and down the stairs, running to find her younger brother and sisters.

Alex clattered down the steps behind Bridget. Now was her big chance. She would get a good look at those boys so she could identify them to the police. But wait a minute! Even if she got a good look at the boys, how would she know their names or where they lived? There was only one thing to do. She would have to follow them and see where they lived.

Alex hurried to catch up with Bridget. She found her in the kitchen with the younger children. They were frightened. A flying rock had narrowly missed one of the twins.

"I'm going to put a stop to this right now!" Alex shouted angrily. "I'm going to follow those boys and find out who they are, and then I'm going to report them to the police."

"But, Alex," Bridget gasped in surprise and fear. "What if they catch you following them? They might beat you up or something."

"Don't worry, I'll be careful," Alex replied. She quickly left the room and sneaked outside through the back door.

Holding her breath and hiding behind trees and bushes, Alex carefully made a wide circle around the house until she was several yards behind the boys. She ducked behind some bushes at the side of the gravel lane. She was now in a position between the boys and the front gate. All she had to do was wait until they decided to leave and then follow them.

Footsteps soon crunched in the lane. Alex risked a quick peek. It was the boys, all right. She concentrated on their faces. She wanted to remember every detail for the police.

Both boys were tall and had long, scraggly dark hair. They wore dirty jeans with big rips in them and black, heavy metal T-shirts. Alex wrinkled her nose in disgust. These were just the kind of boys she tried to avoid. She wriggled further down behind the bushes. She did not want them to catch her.

"Hey, Sims, wait up!" one of the boys called to his companion. He stopped right in front of Alex's bush. He pulled out a cigarette and a book of matches.

Alex turned up her nose as tobacco fumes polluted the air around her.

"Hey, let me have a cigarette," the other boy demanded. Soon, Alex was fighting the urge to cough and choke as smoke from the two cigarettes filled her mouth and nose.

The boys moved on down the lane. Alex stumbled out of the bushes, determined to follow them and find out where they lived. She now knew that one of the boys was called Sims. She wondered if that was his last name or just a nickname.

The boys soon turned off of the lane and hopped over a low place in the old stone wall. Alex waited a few moments and then cautiously followed them across the neighboring backyards. She hoped they wouldn't turn around and see her.

A sudden barking startled Alex. A dog had run to the end of a fence and was barking loudly at her. Alex tried to hush the dog but it kept on barking. She hurried past the fence.

Looking ahead, Alex saw the two boys disappear around the corner of a house. Slowing her pace, Alex carefully and quietly reached the house and then peeked around the corner. There was no sign of the boys.

Moving forward, Alex had almost reached the front of the house when a long, skinny arm grabbed her from behind! She was roughly shoved up against the house. Alex stared into the angry eyes of the boy called Sims.

"Why are you following us?" the boy demanded. He held one of her arms so tightly that Alex winced in pain.

"You better answer him," his companion suddenly appeared. He blew cigarette smoke in Alex's face.

Alex coughed and struggled harder. Sims twisted her arm painfully behind her back.

Alex cried out. Tears came to her eyes. "Stop it!" she screamed.

"Shut up!" the boys hissed. They looked nervously about them. "Come with us," they ordered and pushed Alex ahead of them, the one boy still gripping her arm. They walked toward the street in front of the house. As they passed the driveway, Alex focused on the mailbox. Written in big letters was the name, SIMS.

Stumbling across the driveway, Alex managed to jerk her arm away from Sims. She kicked at him and at the same time screamed at the top of her lungs. The front door of the house next door suddenly opened. A large, burly man stepped out onto his front porch.

"What do you think you're doing?" the man yelled at the two boys.

Immediately, the boys let go of Alex

and turned to face the man. He angrily pointed a finger at the boys.

Alex did not wait to hear what the man had to say. Seizing the chance to escape, she turned and fled down the street as fast as she could go!

At the end of the street, Alex did not slow down but turned a corner and ran up another street. Afraid that the boys might follow her, she ran through backyards and climbed over fences.

Finally, after running for what seemed like hours and hours, Alex collapsed in the grass beside a small neighborhood park. Gasping for breath, tears suddenly sprang to her eyes. She was completely lost and did not know what to do.

CHAPTER 6

Lost and Found

Alex picked herself up and brushed the tears from her eyes. She stumbled into the park and over to the nearest swing set. Taking a seat on one of the swings, Alex tried to think what to do.

She took a good look all around the park and then at the street that surrounded the park. Nothing looked familiar. She had no idea where she was.

One by one, lights blinked on in the nearby houses. It was almost dark, and Alex was getting more and more afraid.

"Dear Lord Jesus," she prayed, "please show me what to do. I am lost and I need to find my way home. Amen."

As Alex stared at the brightly lit houses all around her, she suddenly knew what God wanted her to do. She should go to one of the houses and use a telephone to call home.

"Thank You, Lord!" Alex cried. She leapt out of the swing and ran over to the street. She knew just which house to go to—the one on the corner with the many lights shining through the windows. It looked extra friendly.

Taking a deep breath, Alex walked up the steps of the brightly lit house and onto the porch. She rang the bell. Immediately, a nice-looking man about her father's age answered the door.

"Uh, hello," Alex said. "May I use your telephone to call my parents?"

"Are you in trouble?" the man asked with a concerned look.

"I am lost," said Alex simply.

"Please come in," the man invited. He held the door open for Alex. She followed him into the kitchen.

The man's wife and children were seated at the kitchen table eating dinner.

"I'm sorry," Alex said, red-faced. "I didn't mean to disturb your dinner."

"Oh, that's all right," said the woman. "Please feel free to use our telephone"

Alex dialed her phone number. When her father answered, she told him what had happened and gave him the address from where she was calling. Her father came to get her immediately. He was very upset. As soon as they got home, Father called the police.

A police officer came to the house to hear Alex's story. Alex recognized her as Officer Fawcett, one of the officers that had come to Bridget's house the day the children's bicycles had been stolen. Alex was glad. She had liked the officer's kindly manner.

The officer sat in the living room with Alex and her family and wrote down everything that Alex told her. Everyone listened quietly until Alex mentioned

the name on the mailbox of the house where the two boys had cornered her.

"SIMS!" her sister exclaimed. "I bet it's Marty Sims. He goes to my school, and he's really bad!"

Everybody stared at Barbara.

"Do you know where Marty Sims lives?" Officer Fawcett asked Barbara.

"No, but his address must be in the school directory," said Barbara. She ran to get it. As soon as she found the address, she gave it to Officer Fawcett.

"Well, it's in the area that Alex described," Officer Fawcett observed. "It sounds like Marty Sims might be one of the boys that tried to hurt Alex today."

"And threw rocks at Bridget's house," Alex added.

"And stole our bicycles!" cried Rudy.

"I will go talk to Marty Sims and his parents tonight," the officer promised.

After she left the house, Alex called Bridget and told her what had happened.

"Oh, I'm so glad you got away from those awful boys," exclaimed Bridget. "But I'm really sorry that you got lost."

"Oh, well," Alex shrugged it off, "at least I'm home now. What about you? The last time I saw you, there was a sofa stuck on your stairway."

"It's still stuck," Bridget laughed. "Mom and I tried to move it, but it's too heavy."

"Maybe my dad could help," Alex said.

When Father heard about the sofa, he immediately volunteered his help. In fact, the entire Brackenbury family

74

decided to go with him. Father brought along Barbara's school directory.

When they reached Bridget's house, the family joined Bridget and her mother on the stairway and pushed and shoved until they moved the sofa down the stairs and into the sun room. They visited with Grandpa for a little while and then inspected the window that had been broken that afternoon by the teenage boys.

"Oh, I sure hope they catch those boys," said Mrs. Lyons, Bridget's mother. "They have broken my windows and scared my children so badly."

"The police are supposed to be talking to one of them tonight," said Father. "Maybe he will give the name of the other boy and they will confess to breaking your windows and stealing my children's bicycles."

After leaving Bridget's house, Father pulled out Barbara's school directory and looked up the address of Marty Sims's house. He decided to drive by it.

The house was not easy to find. The

neighborhood seemed to be made up of circular streets and dead ends. More than once, Father had to turn the car around.

"I see now why you got so lost this afternoon, Firecracker," he said to Alex. "These streets are very confusing."

Finally, Father found the right street. He drove slowly until he found the house.

"That's it!" Alex shouted as soon as she saw the mailbox with the name SIMS painted on it.

"So it was Marty Sims," Barbara said disgustedly. "It figures!"

"Well, it looks like the police are handling it now," said Father. He pointed to the police car parked in the driveway.

"I hope they get the name of the other boy," said Mother. "Those boys should be punished."

"Yeah, and I hope the police find our bicycles," added Alex.

"Don't count on it too much," Father warned. "If the boys did steal the bicycles, I don't think they would have brought them to their houses. I think they would have hidden them somewhere else."

Alex's heart sank at those words. She had hoped the police would find the bicycles tonight at Marty Sims's house, but her father was probably right. More than likely, the bikes had been hidden, and the police wouldn't find them right away.

Father turned the car around and drove home. It was quite late when they reached home. Alex went to bed immediately and dreamed about bicycles, broken windows, and boys in black T-shirts.

The next day, Alex and Bridget told their friends Janie, Julie, and Lorraine all about the events of the night before.

"I wish I had been there," complained Janie. "I always miss all the good stuff!"

"The good stuff?" Alex exclaimed. "You call getting lost and almost getting killed by two boys good stuff?"

"Well, no," Janie replied, "but I bet it was exciting."

The girls laughed.

"At least now the police will punish those boys and make them stop throwing rocks," said Julie.

"I don't think so," Alex shook her head.

"What do you mean?" the others asked.

"Well, my dad says the police probably won't be able to do anything to the boys for throwing rocks," answered Alex.

"Why not?" the others demanded.

"They would have to catch them in the act . . . you know, actually catch the boys on Bridget's property before they could do anything to them."

"You mean those boys can come back and throw rocks at our windows again?" Bridget asked in amazement.

"Yes, until someone proves they are breaking the windows," Alex explained.

"But we saw them do it," cried Bridget.

"No good," Alex told her. "We're just a bunch of kids, and it's our word against theirs."

"But that's not fair!" the other girls exploded.

"That's what my dad says," Alex shrugged, "and since he's an attorney, he ought to know."

That night Alex learned that her father, indeed, had been right. Marty Sims had refused to confess to the crime. The police did not have the name of the other boy. There was no way to prove who had broken Bridget's windows.

"I know it's wrong," Father told Alex, "but sometimes criminals go free."

"What about the boys grabbing Alex and threatening her?" Mother asked. "Won't the police do anything about that?"

"According to the police, Marty Sims claimed that Alex was trespassing on his property and he had a right to question her," Father replied.

"But can't we do anything about them breaking Bridget's windows?" Alex wanted to know. She had given up on finding her bicycle.

"Not unless they are caught in the act of breaking the windows," said Father.

Feeling very frustrated, Alex stomped her way upstairs, lay down on her bed, and stared at the ceiling. Her black dog, T-Bone, joined her on the bed.

"What can we do, T-Bone?" Alex rubbed the labrador's big head. He had stretched his head across her stomach. "There must be something we can do."

She thought for a few moments, then Alex suddenly sat straight up in bed, upsetting T-Bone. "I got it! I got it!" she hugged the dog excitedly. "I gotta go call Bridget!"

She leapt to her feet and ran to her sister's room. For once, Barbara was not talking on the telephone. Alex dialed Bridget's number and waited impatiently for someone to answer.

"Hello," said Bridget's voice on the other end of the line.

"Bridget!" Alex exclaimed. "Do you have a camera? I've got a great idea how to catch those boys red-handed!"

CHAPTER 7

An Icy Bath

The next day at morning recess, Alex told her friends how she planned to catch the teenagers who had broken so many of Bridget's windows.

"You mean you're going to take their pictures?" Janie exclaimed when she heard Alex's plan.

"Exactly!" Alex nodded her head. "If we take pictures of them throwing rocks at Bridget's house, the police will have to do something about it. That will be the evidence that they need."

"That's a great idea," Bridget decided.

"Yeah, but how are you going to take their pictures?" asked Julie. "They're not exactly going to stand there and smile and say, 'CHEESE!' "

The other girls laughed.

"We'll just have to be sneaky," Alex replied, "and take their pictures without them knowing it."

"Sounds risky to me," said Lorraine.

"Sounds exciting to me," declared Janie. "Count me in. I'm not going to miss the excitement this time."

"Me, neither," the others agreed.

"Great!" said Alex. "Does anybody have a camera we can use?"

"I lost mine at camp last summer," said Janie sadly.

"I have a camera you could use," offered Julie, "but it doesn't have any film in it."

"Well, maybe we could buy some film for it," Alex suggested. "How much does film cost anyway?"

"Only a couple of dollars," replied Julie, "but I'm broke right now."

"We'll all pitch in," Alex said cheerfully. "I have an extra dollar at home."

"I have money too," said Lorraine.

"Then let's all meet at Bridget's house tomorrow after school," said Alex. "Bring any extra money you have, and we'll walk to a store and buy a roll of film for Julie's camera."

"What store are we going to walk to?" asked Janie.

"I dunno," Alex shrugged. "What's the closest store to your house?" she asked Bridget.

"There's a grocery store a couple of blocks away," Bridget replied. "You can get film there."

"Great!" Alex responded. "We'll show those boys that they can't break your windows and get away with it!"

After school the following day, the girls walked to Bridget's house. They were accompanied by Rudy, Jason, and Bridget's younger brother and sisters. It was a beautiful fall day and everyone was excited.

"Hey, I know what we should do!" Janie called out to the others. "Whoever takes the pictures of the boys should hide up in a big, tall tree, and then when they come along, SNAP! the pictures are taken!"

"And, of course, we all know that it will be you up in the big, tall tree," Alex teased Janie.

Everyone laughed. They knew that Janie was afraid to climb trees.

When the children arrived at Bridget's house, Bridget went to check on her grandfather. She told him that she and the others were going for a walk to the grocery store.

Before they left, Alex counted all the money that they had brought with them. She had brought a dollar and so had Lorraine. Janie had brought two quarters and a dime. Julie had brought no money, but she had her camera. She handed it to Alex.

"Awesome," Alex exclaimed as she looked through the lens of the camera. "I can't wait to take pictures of those boys!"

"Then we'll turn 'em over to the police

and be heroes!" cried Rudy.

"That's right! We'll catch the criminals red-handed," laughed Alex. She handed the camera back to Julie and bundled all the money into a coin purse. She started to slip it into her pocket, but Rudy stopped her.

"Can Jason and I carry the money?" he asked.

"I don't think so," Alex told him. "What if you drop it or something?"

"We won't drop it," the boys assured her. "We'll put it in our pockets. Please, can we carry it?"

"Oh, okay," Alex gave in. She handed the coin purse to Rudy who promptly stuck it into his jeans pocket.

"I'll carry the money halfway and then you can carry it the rest of the way," he told Jason.

The children started on their journey to the store. It was quite a jolly and excited group. Alex, Rudy, and Jason took the lead. Then came Bridget and

85

her brother Peter, and her younger sisters, Sarah and Sandra. Last of all came Janie, Julie, and Lorraine.

The children skipped up the street and crossed to another street, laughing and talking as they went. Everything was fine until they came to a bridge that crossed over a rather large creek. The bridge was high and arched with several steps leading up to it from the sidewalk.

"Neat!" Rudy exclaimed when he saw the bridge. He began to run for it.

"Wait, Rudy!" Jason yelled after his best friend. "Give me the money now! It's my turn to carry it!"

"Wait 'til we get over the bridge," Rudy hollered back at Jason.

"No!" Jason shouted. "It's my turn now!"

"Okay," Rudy grumbled. He stopped and fished the coin purse out of his pocket. Without bothering to make a good throw, he tossed it in Jason's direction. The throw was too high and way off target. The coin purse sailed past Jason's outstretched hand and over the guardrails of the bridge.

"Oh, no," everyone cried as they watched the little purse drop to the creek below. It landed on the muddy bank right next to the water's edge.

"Brussels sprouts!" Alex shouted at her brother. "How could you do such a dumb thing?"

"Jason should have caught it," Rudy said as he scowled at his friend.

"Me?" Jason cried. "You threw it way over my head!"

"Well, no matter whose fault it is, we gotta get it," Alex told the boys. "Come on."

She led the way back across the bridge and began to work her way down the slippery bank. It was slow going. Alex had to position each step carefully as she tried hard to keep her balance. Rudy and Jason followed slowly after her.

Inch by inch, Alex moved toward the bottom of the bank and the coin purse that lay at the edge of the creek. She had almost reached it when disaster struck.

A small bush that Rudy was holding onto for balance suddenly gave way. Rudy toppled over backwards and slid into Jason who lost his balance and crashed into Alex. All three children landed KERSPLASH! in the icy creek water!

"YEEEOOOOOWW!" they screamed as they hit the water. Mud and water flew as the children scrambled to get out of the creek. In the mad dash, Alex just barely remembered the coin purse. She reached out and grabbed it just before it sank under the water.

Rudy's shoes, however, were a different matter. When Rudy had fallen into the creek, he had pushed his shoes completely under a thick layer of mud. When he stood up to get out of the water, his feet came out but his shoes stayed behind.

"Help! My shoes have disappeared!" he called to Alex and Jason.

"What do you mean your shoes have disappeared?" Alex snapped at her younger brother. She was cold and wet and covered with mud, and she did not want to hear any of Rudy's silliness.

"Well, look! My shoes are gone!" Rudy insisted.

Alex stared at the muddy hole where Rudy's feet had been. With a big sigh, she leaned over and reached her arm into the mud. Her fingers searched and searched but she could find no trace of the shoes.

"Brussels sprouts, what happened to 'em?" she cried in frustration.

"What's the matter?" Bridget called down from the bridge.

"We can't find Rudy's shoes!" Alex hollered.

"Yeah, my shoes have drowned!" Rudy announced to the group on the bridge.

There was an outbreak of giggles. Even Alex had to smile at Rudy's joke.

Taking a big stick, Alex poked through the water and mud at the edge of the creek. It was no use. She just could not find Rudy's shoes. Tired, wet, and cold, she gave up the search.

"What am I going to tell Mom about my shoes?" Rudy wailed as Alex pushed him and Jason back up the steep bank to the bridge.

"You'll just have to tell her that you lost your shoes in the mud," Alex replied. "Even if we had found them, they probably would have been ruined in all that mud."

As soon as she reached the bridge once more, Alex pulled off her wet shoes and rubbed her frozen feet. She was soaked to the knees. Rudy and Jason were not any better off. They hopped from one foot to the other.

"Are you freezing?" Bridget asked Alex in concern.

"Yes," Alex declared. She frowned at Rudy and Jason. But soon she had to laugh. The boys were covered with mud and looked absolutely ridiculous. Rudy's blond hair was streaked with brown, and Jason's face was dotted with mud freckles.

"Do I look as bad as you do?" Alex giggled at the boys. Soon, they were all laughing about their mud bath.

"Should we just go back home and forget about getting the film for the camera today?" Bridget finally asked Alex.

"How far is the store?" Alex asked. She did not want to give up their plan no matter how miserable she felt.

"It's not very far," Bridget answered.

"It's just another block from the bridge."

"Oh, come on. We can make it," Alex told the others.

"Did you get the coin purse?" Julie asked Alex.

"Oh, yeah," Alex pulled it out of her pocket. The dollar bills were wet but undamaged.

The children hurried across the bridge as fast as Alex, Rudy, and Jason could hobble. Finally reaching the grocery store, Alex handed Bridget the coin purse. Everyone went inside the store except Alex, Rudy, and Jason. They were too muddy and had to stay outside.

Passersby stared at the three children as they dripped water and mud outside the front door of the grocery store. Alex ignored the stares and tried to act as if she always stood around with her feet and legs covered with mud. She turned her back to the sidewalk and stared at people's reflections in the big glass window in the front of the store.

Suddenly, what she saw in one of the reflections made her stiffen in surprise.

A long-haired boy in a black T-shirt passed immediately behind Alex on the sidewalk. Alex recognized him instantly. It was Sims!

Sims either did not see Alex or did not recognize her as she stood with her back to him. Slowly turning her head, Alex watched Sims as he strolled down the sidewalk, a cigarette in one hand. With the other hand he pushed a bicycle. There was something very strange about Sims and the bicycle. It didn't take Alex very long to figure out what it was. Sims was pushing a pink, girl's bicycle!

"I bet he just stole that bike!" Alex exclaimed out loud.

"Huh?" Rudy and Jason were puzzled by Alex's outburst.

"Stay here!" she ordered the boys. Alex, very quietly and very patiently began to follow Sims down the sidewalk.

CHAPTER 8

A Narrow Escape

"I wonder where Sims is taking that bicycle?" Alex asked herself as she silently trailed the teenager from the grocery store down the sidewalk, across the street, and around a bend in the road. Sims stopped suddenly at a driveway. Alex leapt behind some bushes a moment before he turned around to see if anyone was following him.

Sims pushed the bicycle up the driveway. He knocked on the garage door. Almost immediately, the garage door opened. Alex caught a glimpse of another long-haired boy. Then Sims, the bicycle, and the other boy disappeared inside the garage. The garage door closed.

"Brussels sprouts!" Alex exclaimed excitedly to herself. Had she found Sims's stolen bicycle hideout? Perhaps her bicycle was in that garage.

For several minutes, Alex kept watch on the garage. When nothing more happened, she decided to hurry back to the store and let her friends know what she had found.

Alex found them waiting anxiously in front of the grocery store. When she told them about Sims and the garage, her friends became excited.

"Let's go see the garage!" Janie cried. She started to run off in that direction, but Alex stopped her.

"No!" Alex told Janie. "We have to be really careful. We can't let Sims know that we have found his hiding place."

"What do you think we ought to do?" Bridget asked Alex.

"Well," Alex considered. "I think we ought to watch for Sims every day and see how many bicycles he takes to the garage."

"We could even take pictures of him with the bicycles," Julie suggested.

"Great idea!" Alex exclaimed. "But we can't let him see us taking the pictures."

"Then we should take the pictures to the police," added Janie.

"Yeah, maybe," said Alex. "But first, I want to be sure that there really are stolen bicycles in that garage before we call the police. I don't want to call them this time until I have some evidence."

"But how are you going to make sure there are stolen bicycles in that garage?" asked Janie.

"I'll just have to get in there some-how, I guess," Alex replied thoughtfully.

"ALEX!" Janie shouted in alarm. "You're not planning on going in there, are you?"

"Shhh!" Alex quieted her friend. "I'll wait until it's safe. I just want to look in that garage before I call the police and tell them it's full of stolen bicycles."

Alex took each of her friends, one by one, back along the sidewalk to the garage where Sims had taken the bicycle. The children hid behind the bushes and were very careful not to be seen. Not once did Sims or the other boy reappear. The garage seemed deserted from the outside.

It was getting late, so the children gave up the watch for that day. They did decide, however, to keep watch on the garage the next day and for as many days as it took to catch Sims at his bicycle stealing business.

For the rest of the week the children took turns watching for Sims. Two of them would hide in the bushes across the street from the old garage while the rest of them waited in front of the grocery store where Alex had first seen Sims. The plan was that whenever the children at the grocery store saw Sims with a bicycle, they would blow a whistle to alert the children keeping watch in the bushes across the street from the garage.

It was Thursday afternoon. Alex and Bridget sat under the bushes across from Sims's garage. Alex clutched Julie's camera. She was hot and sweaty and tired of waiting for Sims.

"I wonder if he'll ever show up," Alex complained to Bridget. "He hasn't come back for three days. Maybe he saw us watching the place and decided not to come back at all."

"No, I don't think he saw us," Bridget replied. "We were careful not to be seen. Maybe he's out looking for bicycles to steal."

Alex sighed and leaned her back against a prickly bush. She hoped Bridget was right. Maybe today would be the day that Sims would show up with a stolen bicycle and she could take his picture.

The two girls sat under the bushes and waited. Just as Alex was again ready to give up and call it quits for yet another day, she heard a high-pitched sound that made her sit up and take notice.

"There's the whistle!" Alex nudged Bridget. "That's the signal that Sims is coming!"

With hearts pounding, Alex and Bridget slid further down under the cover of the bushes. They were very quiet, hardly daring to breathe. Alex strained to see through leaves and twigs.

Soon feet crunched on the road beside them, and all at once dirty tennis shoes and a bicycle tire came into view. Holding their breaths, the girls did not move a muscle until the shoes and tire moved away from the bush. Then Alex leaned partway out of the bushes.

"It's Sims, all right!" Alex whispered to Bridget, "and he's got another bike!" Alex positioned the camera carefully and pushed the button to snap a picture of Sims.

CLICK! The camera seemed to make more noise than usual. Perhaps it was because everything else was so quiet.

Whatever the reason, Sims heard it.

Alex and Bridget gasped as the teenager turned with an angry look in their direction. He dropped the bicycle in the middle of the street and strode quickly toward the bushes where Alex and Bridget were hiding.

"RUN FOR IT, BRIDGET!" Alex screamed as Sims dove at the bushes. Still holding the camera, Alex barely escaped by snapping a large branch in the teenager's face. She untangled herself from the bushes and stumbled up the street.

"OW!" Sims hollered when the branch hit his nose. "I'M GONNA TEAR YOU APART!" he yelled at Alex. He did not bother at all with Bridget who lay terrified on the ground below him. Instead, he took off running after Alex. Bridget got up and followed both of them.

Alex ran as fast as she could up the street toward the grocery store where her friends were waiting. Being a softball and soccer player, Alex could run fast. Sims, however, had longer legs and was determined to catch up with her. He ran right at her heels for the two blocks it took to reach the grocery store.

"HEEELLLPPP!" Alex shouted as soon as she rounded the street corner and spotted her friends.

People jumped out of the way as Alex and Sims clattered up the sidewalk in front of the store. Alex could barely focus on the surprised faces of her friends. When she passed Julie, Alex tossed her the camera. Julie managed to catch it before it hit the ground. Sims slid to a stop, not knowing whether to continue chasing Alex or to go for the camera. He did neither, for just at that moment a small figure leapt out of nowhere.

"LEAVE MY SISTER ALONE!" Rudy hollered at the top of his lungs. He barreled into Sims with such force that it knocked the older boy off his feet and into a display of pumpkins that were stacked in front of the grocery store.

"AAAHHHH!" Sims cried as an avalanche of pumpkins crashed down around him. Several broke open and spilled their squishy insides all over Sims. Others rolled out onto the sidewalk and into the street. Pedestrians and cars alike swerved to avoid them.

"What's going on out here?" shouted a red-faced man who ran out the door of the grocery store. He wore a manager's badge. He stood over Sims and glared at the teenager.

Alex grabbed Rudy, and they, Bridget, and the rest of the children quickly retreated down the sidewalk. They ran all the way back to the arched bridge where Alex, Rudy, and Jason had fallen into the water several days before. They ducked out of sight under one of the ends of the bridge and huddled together in a group.

"Brussels sprouts!" Alex gasped. "That was a narrow escape."

"No kidding," agreed Bridget. "I thought Sims was going to murder you!"

"Me, too!" Janie shuddered.

"But Rudy saved the day!" cried Jason. He gave his best friend a pat on the back.

"That was a great move, Rudy," Alex told her brother. "Thanks for getting me out of a jam."

"Aw, sure," Rudy shrugged as if it were nothing.

"Can you believe how all those pumpkins fell on Sims?" Julie laughed.

"Yeah," chuckled Bridget. "I bet he gets in a lot of trouble for wrecking the pumpkin display."

"I bet he gets in so much trouble that the manager will even call the police," declared Janie.

Alex sat up suddenly. Janie had given her an idea. She looked at her friends. "I'm going back to that garage," she told them calmly.

"What?" they all gazed at her as if she were crazy.

"I'm going back there," Alex repeated.

"But Alex, it's too dangerous," Bridget objected.

"If Sims sees you again, he really will murder you!" Janie warned Alex.

"He won't see me," Alex replied. "Right now, Sims is too busy with the grocery store manager. He'll probably be there for a long time, especially if they decide to call the police."

"But why do you want to go back to the garage?" her friends asked.

"Because we need to find out if there really are stolen bicycles in there," Alex explained. "Now that Sims knows we have spotted his hideout, he'll try to move the bikes. If he does, we'll never know where he's hidden them. We won't be able to fool him again. He'll be on the lookout for us now."

"So how do you expect to see the stolen bicycles?" Julie asked. "The garage is all locked up."

"Maybe there's an open back door or an open window," Alex replied. "Anyway, I have to try. Can I use your camera again? We might want some pictures."

"Sure," Julie replied, "but we're going with you."

"No!" Alex said. "Only one of us should go. A big group would be seen too easily."

"But we can't let you go back there by yourself," protested Bridget. "It's too dangerous."

"I'll be careful," Alex promised. "I'll just slip in and slip out again. It'll be simple!"

"Well, I don't like it," Janie declared. "What if you run into trouble and need help?"

"That's where you come in," Alex told her friend. "I want you to go back to Bridget's house and wait for me. If I don't show up back there in an hour, call the police. Tell them all that's happened and have them come to the garage."

"What if the police don't believe us?" Janie wanted to know.

"Make them believe you," Alex said firmly. "Tell them that it's a very dangerous place and that I've been trapped there."

"Okay," her friends agreed reluctantly. They watched as Alex stood up and slipped Julie's camera in her pocket. Then without saying another word, Alex crawled out from under the bridge and began the dangerous journey back to Sims's garage.

CHAPTER 9

A Daring Idea

Alex avoided the grocery store as she hurried back to the garage. In fact, she avoided that entire street, choosing instead to approach the garage from a back way. Keeping a sharp lookout for Sims, Alex reached the garage.

The place looked abandoned. High weeds grew in clumps around the building. Old, rusted trash cans stood at odd angles at the back door. Swatting away insects, Alex waded through the tall weeds to the door. She tried to turn the knob, but it wouldn't budge.

There was a small window high above and to the left of the back door. It was the old-fashioned crank style. The glass swung to the outside when the window was opened. Alex could see that it was slightly open.

Balancing on one of the rusted trash cans, Alex stretched for the window. She grabbed hold of the dirty glass and pulled on it until it opened wide enough for her to squeeze through the opening. After batting away the first layer of cobwebs, Alex boosted herself up to the window.

It was a tight fit, but she managed to wiggle through the opening. Piles of dirt cascaded down when Alex finally dropped to the floor below. She was inside Sims's garage!

Forcing her eyes to focus in the dim light, Alex smiled to herself. She had been right. The entire garage was filled with all different types and styles of bicycles. They had to be stolen!

Pulling out Julie's camera, Alex began snapping pictures of the bicycles. She moved to different areas of the garage, wanting to take pictures of all the bicycles. She had to hurry. Sims might come back at any moment.

Focusing through the lens of the camera for yet another picture, Alex saw something that almost made her drop the camera in surprise. There, right in front of her, stood her own bicycle! She had been so busy taking pictures that she had not thought to look for it.

Rushing to her bicycle, Alex gave it a quick inspection. It was hers all right! She found the small dent that she had made when she had accidentally dropped it one day. She remembered how upset she had been to put the first dent in her new bike.

Alex was excited to find her bicycle. It was like discovering an old friend that had been lost for years. She sat on the seat and imagined coasting down the city streets.

After a few imaginary moments, however, Alex remembered her dangerous situation. She had better get out of the garage quickly before Sims returned. If only she could get her bicycle out of the garage too. She could ride it home. What better evidence would she need than her own stolen bicycle to show the police? They would have to believe her!

Alex tried to open the back door from the inside, but it seemed permanently stuck. Now she was faced with a problem. To get her bicycle out, she would have to open the big garage door at the front of the garage. What if Sims's buddy was watching the garage? He would surely notice if Alex opened the big door.

Alex walked over to the door and peeked through the curtain that hung over its rectangular window. What she saw made her gasp in surprise. A large van was pulling into the driveway. Inside the van were Sims and his buddy!

Alex froze. What should she do? She looked in panic for a place to hide.

In one corner of the garage beside a pile of lumber scraps stood a large, empty barrel. Not seeing a better hiding place at the moment, Alex scrambled inside the barrel. She ducked down out of sight just as the garage door squeaked and groaned its way open.

"WHEW!" Alex heard Sims exclaim as he and his friend entered the garage and pulled the garage door shut with a bang. "I thought I'd never get away from that grocery store!"

"You sure smell like pumpkin," his friend laughed.

"Shut up!" growled Sims. "You'd smell like pumpkin too if a bunch had fallen on you."

"They didn't just fall on you," his friend continued to laugh. "They broke all over you. You have pumpkin seeds in your hair."

"I said SHUT UP!" Sims hollered. He stomped his foot angrily. "Wait until I catch those kids. I'll make them wish they'd never messed with me!"

"Yeah, especially that one girl that we caught hanging around your house a couple weeks ago," his friend added. "I told you we should have taken care of her back then."

"I'll take care of her all right," threatened Sims. "Just wait 'til I get my hands on her!"

Huddled in the barrel, Alex tried to keep from shaking. She was afraid her teeth might rattle so loudly that the boys would hear her. She listened to Sims yell and complain about the pumpkins. It seemed that Sims had had to pay for the damaged pumpkins himself.

Sims and his buddy went on yelling and shouting. Alex shivered inside the barrel and tried to stay quiet. She tried to guess how long she had been in the garage. It seemed like more than an hour. Surely her friends had called the police by now. That was her only hope.

"We better start loading the bikes into the van," Sims suddenly told his friend. "Since those kids know about this garage, we'll have to take the bikes to another hiding place."

Alex heard the garage door squeak open again. She very cautiously peeked out of the top of the barrel. She caught her breath in alarm. Sims and the other boy were rapidly pushing the bicycles toward the van and stacking them inside. What should she do? She couldn't let them get away this time!

Alex looked for her bicycle. There it was, still parked in the garage. It wasn't too far away from the barrel.

Suddenly, Alex had a daring idea. She

could jump on her bicycle and ride right past the two boys. Surely they would follow her. She could draw them away and maybe, just maybe, the police would have time to get to the garage. She had to try. There was nothing else to do. "Help me, Lord Jesus," she quickly prayed.

Silently, Alex climbed out of the barrel. Tipping it over on its side, she pushed the barrel right into the bunch of bicycles parked around the van.

CRASH! The bicycles fell in all different directions. Some even rolled backwards into the street.

"HEY!" Sims and his buddy yelled in surprise. They looked up as Alex peddled furiously past them on her bicycle.

Sims made a giant swipe at Alex, but she ducked and sped down the driveway. Sims jumped onto the closest bicycle and took off after Alex. The other teenager did the same thing.

Alex waited for them at the intersection. She let them almost catch up with her. She wasn't worried. Nobody could catch her when she was riding her new ten-speed bike!

When the teenagers had almost reached her, Alex whipped her bicycle around the corner. She gasped! A police car was heading straight for her!

Alex swerved and toppled into a ditch. The police car squealed to a stop. Sims and his friend could not stop their bikes in time. BLAM! They slammed into the front end of the police car. Sims flew off his bike and onto the hood of the car. He stared through the windshield at the two officers inside the car.

"HALT!" one of the police officers cried as he jumped out of the car. He grabbed the two boys and made them stand in front of the car.

The other police officer climbed down into the ditch to help Alex. "Are you all right?" she asked. Alex looked up and grinned. It was Officer Fawcett!

"Well, well," Officer Fawcett chuckled.

"It looks like we caught those boys this time."

"Yeah, and there's a garage full of stolen bicycles right around the corner," Alex told her, waving her hand in the right direction. "And look," she added, "this is my bicycle that was stolen!"

Officer Fawcett looked surprised. She followed Alex to the garage. There she saw all the bicycles, some in the garage, some outside, and some partly packed into the van.

"Wow!" Officer Fawcett whistled. "Looks like we caught some big bicycle thieves." She gave Alex a pat on the shoulder.

The other officer caught up with them and rolled the police car into the driveway behind the van. Sims and his friend sat unhappily handcuffed in the backseat.

The police officers called Alex's parents. It wasn't long before the Brackenbury station wagon also pulled into the driveway. Alex grinned as her parents,

Barbara, Rudy, Jason, Bridget, Janie, Julie, and Lorraine all piled out of the car.

"Alex!" they cried in relief as soon as they saw her.

"Hey, our bikes!" hollered Rudy and Jason. They immediately started to pull them from a pile of bicycles. A police officer stopped them.

"Sorry," he said. "We'll need your bicycles for evidence. We'll give them back to you in a few days."

Mother and Father gave Alex a big hug. "So you were right about Sims and the bicycles all along," said Mother.

"Yeah, Alex, you're a hero!" cried Rudy.

"Shhhh!" Alex tried to quiet her brother.

"Yes, she is a hero," agreed Officer Fawcett coming over to stand by Alex. "We're all very grateful to her for catching the bicycle crooks."

"And we're all very proud of you, Firecracker," added Father.

"Aw, it was nothing," said Alex,

embarrassed by all the attention.

"Nothing?" cried Janie. "I want to hear how you did it."

"Yes, tell us all about it," her friends asked.

Alex told everyone how she had crawled through the garage window and hid in the barrel from Sims and his friend. She told how she had escaped from the garage on her bicycle and how the two boys had run smack into the police car and been caught by the police.

"Wow, what a story," her friends and family exclaimed. "That ought to be on the news."

"I wouldn't be surprised if it is," commented Officer Fawcett. She winked at Alex.

Sure enough, it wasn't long before a car from one of the local television stations pulled into the driveway. A reporter and photographer jumped out of the car.

Alex told her story to the reporter while the photographer rolled the camera.

The reporter then talked to Officer Fawcett. The photographer shot pictures of the pile of bicycles. Sims and his friend glared through the police car window as their pictures were taken.

That night Alex watched herself on television. It was hard to believe that the whole thing was real. To think that Sims had been caught and her bicycle would be returned in a few days was almost too good to be true! But when the telephone started ringing, Alex knew it had to be true. It seemed like everyone they knew called to congratulate Alex. The phone did not quit ringing until late that night.

Tired but happy, Alex finally crawled into bed. Before she went to sleep, she remembered the most important thing that she had to do. Getting out of bed once more, she got down on her knees.

"Thank You, Lord Jesus, for answering my prayer. Thank You for helping me catch Sims and for keeping me safe. I pray in Your name. Amen."

CHAPTER 10

The Real Treasure

Alex was a hero at school the next day. Everyone had seen her on television. That seemed to be all anyone could talk about. Even children she did not know spoke to her in the hallways and in the lunchroom. At recess, Alex was bombarded with questions from eager schoolmates wanting to know more about her adventures. Even the teachers crowded around her.

Alex enjoyed being the center of attention, but when she got home, she had an even bigger thrill. Officer Fawcett was waiting for her.

"Hello, Alex," the officer smiled when Alex walked in the door. "I have a surprise for you."

"Really?" Alex's eyes lit up.

"The people in our department want to give you something for your help in catching the bicycle thieves. Can you tell me what you would like for a reward?"

"You mean anything I want?" Alex asked.

"Well, I don't think we can give you Royals Stadium," answered Officer Fawcett with a wink. "Perhaps we could manage something smaller though."

Alex thought for a moment. For some reason she could not explain, a picture of Bridget's grandfather popped into her mind.

"I know what I want!" she suddenly exclaimed. "I want a wheelchair!"

"A what?" questioned Officer Fawcett, completely surprised.

"It's for Bridget's grandpa," Alex explained. "He can't walk, and it's too hard for Bridget or her mother to lift him out of bed. Oh, a wheelchair would be perfect!" she clapped her hands. "But would that be too expensive?" she asked a moment later.

"I'll see what we can do," Officer Fawcett replied. She shook her head in disbelief. "You are truly an amazing girl."

Even after the bicycle episode was over, Alex continued to walk over to Bridget's house after school. Bridget had become a very good friend.

The girls kept busy. They put the finishing touches on the sun room. They dusted and polished the furniture and arranged dried flowers and leaves in vases around the room. It was such a warm, happy room. They loved to just sit in it and talk.

Then one evening, Officer Fawcett called Alex. She asked if Alex and her family could meet her at Bridget's house the next evening.

"Bridget and her family know I am coming," Officer Fawcett told Alex, "but I did not tell them that you were going to come, and I did not tell them about the wheelchair. I wanted to surprise them."

"You mean you got a wheelchair?" Alex asked hopefully.

"Yes, we did," Officer Fawcett replied.

"Brussels sprouts!" Alex cried joyfully.

After her talk with Officer Fawcett, Alex danced around the kitchen. "Whoopee!" she cried and tossed Mother's dish towel in the air. She did a little dance with T-Bone until he barked so loud she had to stop.

"I'm so glad Officer Fawcett got a wheelchair for Grandpa!" Alex said to her parents as she collapsed in a kitchen chair beside them.

"We think that what you have done, honey, is wonderful," said Mother giving Alex a hug.

"Yes, Firecracker, giving your reward to Grandpa is a true act of love," said Father.

"Well," Alex shrugged her shoulders,

"I guess I will store up some more heavenly treasure."

"Indeed you will," Father replied with a smile. He put his arm around Alex and squeezed her tight. "That's the best kind of treasure you'll ever have."

The next day at school, Alex could hardly keep from telling Bridget about the wheelchair. She could not wait for the day to be over.

Finally, it was time to go to Bridget's house. Janie, Julie, and Lorraine were going too. So was Jason. Alex wanted everyone to share in the joy that night.

When they got to Bridget's house, Officer Fawcett opened the door. She smiled broadly at Alex and her family and friends.

"Come in," she held open the door for them.

"Where is everybody?" Alex asked. The usual chatter was missing. The big house was unusually quiet.

"They are all waiting in Grandpa's

room," Officer Fawcett told her. "I asked them to stay there. I told them that I had a surprise for them. I think you ought to push the wheelchair into the room."

"Really?" Alex clapped her hands together excitedly. She couldn't wait to see the look of surprise on the family's faces. "Where is the wheelchair?" she asked.

"Right behind you," laughed Officer Fawcett.

Alex turned to see several police officers gathered on the front porch of the house. Two of them were carrying a brand-new, shiny wheelchair.

"Oh, this is great!" Alex and her family and friends exclaimed. When the wheelchair was set down, Alex sat in it to test it out.

Officer Fawcett disappeared into the back of the house. Soon she reappeared and motioned everyone to follow her. Alex slowly pushed the wheelchair across the wooden floors to Grandpa's room.

There was stunned silence when Alex

and the wheelchair appeared at the entrance to Grandpa's bedroom. Bridget and her mother stared at Alex with wide-open mouths.

Alex pushed the wheelchair over to Grandpa's bed. "This wheelchair is for you," she told the elderly man. "I got a reward for helping catch the boys who stole our bicycles, and I decided the best thing to do would be to give it to you."

The old man's eyes filled with tears as he listened to Alex. Trembling, he grasped her hands and held them tight. Staring into Grandpa's grateful eyes, Alex knew that she had made the right decision. This was the treasure. This was the treasure that the Lord was storing in heaven for her that very moment. On earth, the treasure could only be known as LOVE.

Cautiously, Grandpa slid out of his bed and onto the seat of the wheelchair. Bridget put slippers on his feet while her mother arranged a small blanket on his lap.

Alex got the honor of being the first one to push Grandpa. They visited the sun room where the girls showed him the special room they had fixed up just for him. They then proceeded to the kitchen where everyone ate Bridget's apple turnovers and cookies provided by the police department. It was a wonderful celebration, and Alex could not remember ever being so happy. She and her family and friends laughed and talked for a long time. Nobody seemed to want to go home. Finally, when it was quite late, everyone said good-bye.

"You know, this might sound funny," Alex told her parents as they drove home from Bridget's house, "but when you do something good for someone, God gives you two treasures."

"Two treasures?" Father asked.

"Yeah," Alex replied. "He not only stores treasure for you in heaven, but He also makes you feel really good while you're still here on earth."

Father laughed. "I bet God has a big treasure chest in heaven just waiting for you, Firecracker. And remember, where your treasure is, there your heart is also."

"Yeah," Alex sighed happily. "I guess my heart is pretty close to heaven right now."

"And that's just where it belongs," said Father.

Amen.